This books is dedicated with love and thanks to Meg Lamond
for her insight and encouragement.

With special thanks to:
Mark Gillmon
Charlie Turner

And thanks to:
Mike Wonnacott
Mark Woodward
Michael Jones

www.veronicalamond.com
Facebook: Landy and Friends
Youtube Channel: Landy and Friends

Under licence from Jaguar Land Rover
This book is not a representation of Jaguar Land Rover or product performance.

# Fender and the Cliff Rescue

Written and illustrated by
Veronica Lamond

Dan and Fender drove up the cliff track to work.

"We need to check the coast path today,
Fender," said Dan. "Part of the cliff has
crumbled away in the storms."

"That looks dangerous!" thought Fender, when he saw the cliff.

Dan put up a barrier to stop people walking on the crumbling steps.

"I'll move the path back to where it's safe to walk," he said.

Dan got out everything he needed for the day's work.

Fender and Scamp made lots of new friends.
Dan cut back the prickly bushes with his loppers.

T589 EAF

The ground was very hard and stoney.
He worked and worked all day long to make the new steps.

On the shore below the waves pounded against the rocks.

Suddenly Fender heard someone shouting.
"Help! Help me!"

"Woof! Woof! Woof!"
barked Scamp.

Matt and Sarah, the lifeguards,
ran across the beach and swam
out to the rescue.

"Thank goodness for that!"
said Fender, watching from the cliff.

"Call the air ambulance!" shouted Matt.
The little girl wasn't well at all.

"Stand back, everyone!" shouted Sarah.
She signalled to the helicopter pilot so he knew where to land.
Sand flew everywhere!

The paramedics soon had the little girl safely
on board.

The helicopter took to the sky.

**"Thwup-thwup-thwup-thwup!"**

Little Scamp whimpered and crouched under Fender.
"Don't be frightened, Scamp," said Fender.
"There they go!" said Dan. "They'll soon be at the hospital."

It was nearly the end of the day.
Dan was very tired and sweaty.

"That's enough work for today,"
he said. "I'll finish the job
tomorrow."

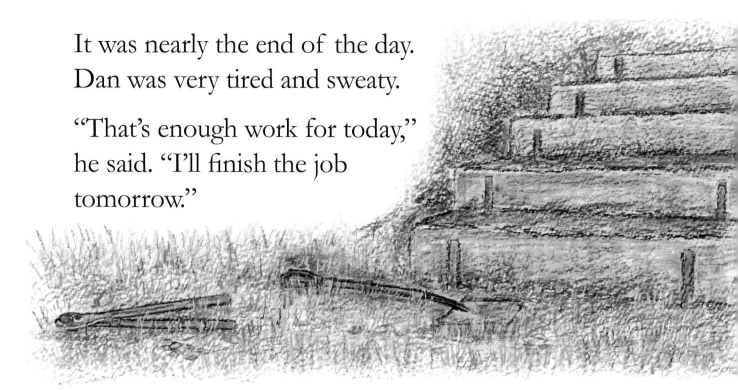

"Hello," said Annie, "I was swimming in the sea and
saw you working up here."

"What a good job you're doing, Dan!" she said.
Fender felt very proud of Dan's hard work.

Annie helped put all the tools in the back of Fender.

Then she had a quick chat with Matt on her phone. "The little girl is recovering well in hospital," he told her.

"That's very good news!" said Dan.

"Let's go for a drive up the coast," suggested Annie. "If we're lucky we might see some puffins on the cliffs."

They drove up the rough hill,

bumpity,

bum**p**!

**bum**p**ity**

Down the steep slope…
clunkety, clunkety **clunk…**

and through the stream, *splish, splash, splosh!*
"This is the life!" laughed Fender as they
lurched along.

When they parked up on the cliff top,
Dan looked through his binoculars.

"Look at all those puffins, Annie!"

But then Dan noticed something else…

Through his binoculars, he saw Jack and Katy
waving wildly at them.

"Come on, Fender, it looks like Jack's in trouble!"

They drove as fast as they could to help...

"We were out walking," said Jack.
"When Molly chased a rabbit
and fell over the edge."

They looked over the cliff.
Molly stared up at them.
She stood shaking
on a narrow ledge.

"I've got my climbing gear and a winch!" said Dan.

He opened Fender's back door. "I'll put Molly in this," he said, pulling out a fishing net.

"You'll need to help me with this rescue, Fender!" said Dan.

He strapped the winch to Fender's chassis then clipped it to his climbing harness.

Annie let out the winch as Dan lowered himself over the edge of the cliff.

Poor Molly whimpered with fear.
She was very glad to see Dan,
but she was too frightened to wag her tail.

The tide was coming in.

Dan gently put her in the
net and attached it to his belt.

"OK! We're ready!" he shouted.
Annie started winding in the winch while Jack gave directions.

"Woof! Woof! Woof!"
barked Scamp, very worried about her friend.

At last Dan and Molly were brought safely up the cliff face.

Jack gave Molly a good rub down with a towel to dry her and warm her up.

"We'll give you a lift to the car park," said Dan.
"Landy will be wondering where you are."

Landy was very pleased to see them all.
"Fender has been a real hero!" said Jack.

"Well done, Fender," said Dan. "You did a rescue just like the helicopter!"

## Books in the Landybook series

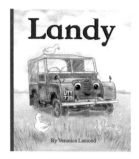

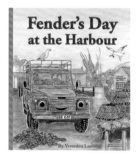

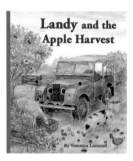
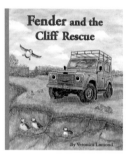

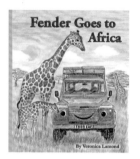

## Also by Veronica Lamond

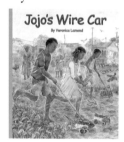

First published in May 2016
By Veronica Lamond

This reprint 2020

© 2016 Veronica Lamond Ltd

Printed by Booths Print  Penryn  Falmouth  Cornwall  UK

ISBN Hardback:  978-0-9935645-0-5
ISBN Paperback:  978-0-9935645-1-2